Born and raised in South Wales, United Kingdom, Alex Thomas is a former student that has a passion for human psychology, dogs and tennis. Coming from an underprivileged background, he has achieved two academic degrees between 2014 and 2019 (BA: English & Contemporary Media; MA: Forensic Linguistics). Since leaving university, he has worked with people to tackle drug and alcohol dependencies and with mental health services.

This book is dedicated to all of my closest friends, family and academic peers who have been a part of and supported my journey through primary, secondary and higher education. It is intended to be enjoyed by all of the above and, furthermore, the thrill seekers both loyal and new to this exciting genre of literature.

Alex J. Thomas

AT NIGHT
THEY WHISPER

AUSTIN MACAULEY PUBLISHERS™

LONDON • CAMBRIDGE • NEW YORK • SHARJAH

Copyright © Alex J. Thomas 2024

The right of Alex J. Thomas to be identified as author of this work has been asserted by the author in accordance with sections 77 and 78 of the Copyright, Designs and Patents Act 1988.

All rights reserved. No part of this publication may be reproduced, stored in a retrieval system, or transmitted in any form or by any means, electronic, mechanical, photocopying, recording, or otherwise, without the prior permission of the publishers.

Any person who commits any unauthorised act in relation to this publication may be liable to criminal prosecution and civil claims for damages.

This is a work of fiction. Names, characters, businesses, places, events, locales, and incidents are either the products of the author'simagination or used in a fictitious manner. Any resemblance to actual persons, living or dead, or actual events is purely coincidental.

A CIP catalogue record for this title is available from the British Library.

ISBN 9781035836055 (Paperback)
ISBN 9781035836062 (ePub e-book)

www.austinmacauley.com

First Published 2024
Austin Macauley Publishers Ltd®
1 Canada Square
Canary Wharf
London
E14 5AA

20240524

I would like to express my sincere gratitude to my mother, Glesni, for her unwavering love, support and loyalty throughout the writing of this book – it is to you I owe so much. Secondly, I would like to thank my sisters, Leanne and Lisa, for their encouragement and humour – you have helped me through rough waters, I am so very proud of you both.

To my friends and academic colleagues, you have shown me the beauty of camaraderie and inspired me to improve in many ways whilst remaining content in others – I thank you always.

A special thank you must go to Marcelle, Tina and Zena for their excellent professionalism in aiding me over the last couple of years – I have learnt so much and I sincerely hope that our paths will continue to cross after our formal time together draws to a close.

Finally, I would like to thank my father, Kevin, for helping me balance my pursuits with joyful, physical activities – you have given me respite through countless snooker and tennis matches.

Table of Contents

"She's Still with Us"

1

As the perpetrator slipped away through the back door, Lyla Kepple lay on her chest on the living room floor, the carpet's thick, synthetic fibres incapable of soaking up the pond that had been created by the blood that oozed from her gaping head wound. Her face tilted and her body barely able to move, one of her nine remaining fingers (one had been cut off) gave one last twitch, the result of sheer willpower. As her breathing became shallower, she closed her eyes and allowed the comforting gas fire to scorch her face, for now, as the beating of her heart slowed and ceased, her body would only get colder.

Whilst her only son, Carl, stepped onto his school bus with his friends and made his journey home, the blood splattered metal stallion used to bludgeon his mother was carefully washed with bleach and polished before being placed on the killer's fireplace, amalgamating with the multitude of other antiques that surrounded it. The stillness of the heavy, ornamental horse aptly mirrored the victim's now lifeless body, that had been left to be discovered by Carl.

Less than an hour separated his mother's murder and Carl's departure from school, timing so precise it could only have been calculated. He wrestled with a group of his friends on the bus; his small, timid frame instinctively backing away when the play got too rough.

'What's wrong, Kepple? Still don't know how to tackle?' one of the boys mocked lightly whilst placing his friend in a headlock.

'Yeah as if,' Carl responded. 'My stop's here anyway,' he said, secretly relieved.

He stood up and went to depart the bus as one of the boys pulled at his hood – a bantering farewell that encapsulated their friendship.

'See you tomorrow for P.E., Kepple,' his friend, Robert, shouted. 'Unless you're afraid of the rugby rumble,' he continued, with an affiliative smile. Carl smiled back at him and chuckled, knowing they all had, for some time, clocked his timidity but at the same time respected him for his macho efforts.

Carl stepped off the bus and started dawdling the five-minute journey to his home, innocently kicking small stones along the way, oblivious to the gruesome scene that awaited him.

2

He approached the house, which was a modest, semi-detached build, a place the Kepples had resided at for nineteen years. He opened the front door and walked inside. With the absence of the smell of cooking food, he immediately sensed something was wrong.

Was mum home? he thought. From the kitchen, his mother would always exclaim, 'How was school?' by the time he had reached the middle of the hallway after arriving home, yet even after closing the front door behind him and walking deep into the passage, he heard but her voice. Before his brain was able to register any more distinct oddities that he had so far encountered, he entered the living room and noticed the gas fire and TV were both on. This was the warm, homely scene he was so accustomed to and he allowed his senses to become satisfied for a few seconds. But upon secondary perception whilst stepping forward, the seemingly reposeful setting had been grossly violated and intruded upon once he noticed his mother lying bloody and lifeless on the floor. The essence of normality carried by the gas fire and TV stood in stark contrast to what was spread out on the floor and his brain scrambled in trying to comprehend the conflicts around him.

He felt himself sink and the saliva dissipate as his mouth dried up.

3

Trembling, the young boy reached for the house phone.

'999 what's the emergency?' said the dispatcher.

'It's my mum, she-she's lying on the floor with blood all over her and … and I don't think she's moving,' Carl stammered. 'There's a gash in her head.'

Quietly too frightened to touch his mother's body and overawed by the urgency of the dispatcher's scientific questions, the twelve-year-old boy ran with the phone next door to inform Yvette and David, who entered the house and immediately rushed the boy back outside, as if to prevent the harrowing scene from becoming instilled in his young and impressionable mind. He stayed standing on the front lawn, comforted by Yvette whilst David spoke to the call handler inside. Clearly evidencing the symptoms of shock, Carl looked up emptily at the paramedics and police who arrived simultaneously shortly afterwards, pronouncing his mother dead at the scene.

Neighbours across the street began to gather in their windows and front gardens at the sight of the ensuing chaos, which was characterised by the emergency services parked outside. Doreen Newman from number six led the speculative atmosphere. She stood in her cleaning apron on the pavement directly opposite the house, pushing up on her tip toes occasionally in an effort to see through the myriad of officers and medics that blocked the Kepple's hallway.

'The car isn't there so Tim *must* be in work,' Doreen deduced, turning to Frank (house number fourteen).

'And that poor kid,' he responded.

'It's the mother. It's got to be,' she said, taking no notice of his reference of sympathy to the young boy. Clearly stimulated by the unfolding drama, she went on: 'If the kid's in the garden and Tim's in work then it's got to be her.'

'So nobody else lives there?' Frank asked curiously, who residing at number fourteen put him somewhat out of the Kepple's immediate neighbouring circle.

'Just those three as far as I've noticed over the last few years. The daughter moved to Brecon with her boyfriend years back.'

'Mm.'

The pair, alongside a handful of other neighbours which were scattered across the street and in their windows, stayed glued to the house, bemused at what could have possibly warranted two police cars and an ambulance which now clogged their cul-de-sac.

A black and yellow, "Police: Do Not Cross" ribbon was placed around the house as the forensic team arrived and investigated the scene. Two police officers approached and took statements from the neighbours.

'Did you see or hear anything suspicious around house number seven this afternoon, particularly around the three o' clock mark?' PC Hartwick asked Doreen Newman and Frank, who were still muttering away opposite the Kepple's house.

'Not a peep,' Frank said. 'I was in the garage seeing to our ol' Vauxhall when I heard the sirens.' He looked at Doreen as a means for her to take her turn.

'I just happened to look out the kitchen window and saw their front door wide open and the boy hammering on Yvette and David's door. He was as pale as a sheet.'

'And you saw nothing before that?' Hartwick asked.

'No, 'fraid not,' she replied. 'Can you tell us what's happened? Is Lyla okay?'

'We can't disclose anything for the moment. Once we know more we'll get back to you.'

PC Hartwick and his colleague questioned the remaining neighbours, to which the information given to them was as expendable as Doreen and Frank's responses – nobody seemed to have noticed anything peculiar at around the presumed time of Lyla's death. After the neighbours' mumblings subsided somewhat, a dark cloud cast itself over the street, as if to indicate that the security and cordiality which had for years been a staple attribute of their community, was suddenly dissipating.

Within the ensuing forty minutes, the boy's father came back from work and clutched at his son tightly on the front lawn, pulling him into his chest.

'I'm so sorry, son,' he said, sobbing. At the loss of her daughter, the boy's grandmother, Pearl, who lived less than a mile away, arrived on foot and gave a feral-like howl as she saw what she knew was her daughter being wheeled out of the house in a body bag. As Carl and his father stood in view of everyone on their front lawn and the body bag shuffled into the back of a black van, the scene seemed to stand still for several seconds for those who had been dispersed across the street for over two hours. It was a culmination to the speculation – Lyla was dead.

4

At 12:30, three days after the murder, two police officers arrived at the Kepple's house to deliver the results from the laboratory and Lyla's post-mortem.

'Please come in,' Tim said expectantly after one of the officers gave three knocks. The father looked dishevelled, and his blemished face carried the suggestion of a few nights of heavy brandy consumption. The two police officers were led through the passage and into the living room, where Pearl and Carl's older half-sister awaited.

'I'm DC Curry and this is my colleague PC Hartwick, who I believe you met at the scene on Monday?'

'Yes. I remember,' Tim said whilst closing the living room door definitively, ensuring his son's prying ears from atop the stairs could not bear witness to any potential morbid details that the officers divulged.

'So have you found the bastard?' Tim asked, indignantly.

'I'm afraid not. Statements we've taken from the locals show that nobody saw anything suspicious around the time of your wife's death and the samples taken from the crime scene showed no foreign DNA or fingerprints.'

'Right?'

'Which indicates that the attacker's skin was likely concealed by some form of clothing.'

'So basically, he was wearing gloves and a mask?' Tim gathered.

'Most likely.'

Tim said nothing and gave a pause as a means of inviting Curry to elaborate on his point.

'Without CCTV in the area or eyewitness accounts, it's all the more difficult. But if we stick with what we're certain of for now, and that's that your wife was attacked from behind and died as a result of blunt force trauma to the head. The coroner's report states that she was hit multiple times and one of her left fingers severed.'

'Monster,' the grandmother interjected stuffily, holding a crumpled tissue in her left hand. At this point, Carl had sneaked a quarter of the way down the stairs but could only bear witness to incoherent mumblings that came from the other side of the closed living room door.

'The metallic horse which you've reported as stolen also gives us cause to believe that the attacker may have used it as a weapon and taken it with them.'

Sarah, Carl's half-sister looked curiously. 'But if he was wearing gloves to … like … prevent any fingerprints, why bother taking the weapon with him?' she asked sharply. 'It just doesn't make sense.'

'Did the horse have any value?' Hartwick asked.

'Hardly. Bloody heavy ol' thing and we're poor buggers. Nothing in here is of value 'cept for what we hold sentimentally,' Tim said.

'Hm-well, it's not uncommon for murderers to take items from their victims as so they can relive the memory of the killing itself.'

'Like a trophy?' Sarah said.

'Yes, that's possible' – but so is a souvenir. Both are common in murder cases, but quite different from one another. We'll make a note and ensure that every pawn shop in the local area keeps an eye out for it.'

'Much appreciated,' Tim said.

'And if there's anything we can do in the meantime, do let us know.' As the living room door opened and the officers escorted out by Tim, Carl tiptoed backwards; his feet expertly avoiding the many creaks embedded on the stairs and landing.

5

Two weeks subsequently, Carl looked in the mirror as he pondered the big day ahead. Dressed in his slightly oversized black suit and Velcro strap school shoes, he left the family car that had followed the hearse and walked towards the church, his grandmother holding one hand and his father the other. They stood outside whilst the two funeral directors bowed in front of the coffin that contained his mother, before pulling her out of the hearse. With some forty people in attendance and ready seated, her coffin travelled steadily towards the altar, its polished wooden material gleaning as the sun pierced through the church windows. Carl fixated on the box, his gaze as still as the body inside.

'A part of her will always be with us, you know,' his grandmother crouched down and whispered. Carl said nothing, continuing to glance towards the coffin with a vacant expression and pale complexion. He clocked a bearer, notably smaller than the other three, trying to mask the strain on his face as they lifted his mother's body onto the stand. 'She's still with us, Carl,' his grandmother reassured again. 'I promise you.' A single teardrop fell from the boy's eye as the last of the hymns were sung and the coffin lowered into the outdoor grounds.

Two days after the funeral, his grandmother took the boy back to her house to stay whilst his father returned to work. She cooked a homemade pie for the pair, as Carl's appetite had begun to improve after initially slumping following his mother's death. He reminisced quietly at the scent of home cooking that much reminded him of when his mother used to prepare food for him after he returned home from school, a smell that he would always remember as being absent on the day he found his mother's body. His grandmother's ageing, grey frame couldn't work with the speed he so often saw his mother use, but she remained efficient, delicately placing both hands into the oven gloves and pulling her effort out of the oven. She distributed the pie into several sections and placed a slice onto his plate, and then her own. Upon serving, Carl began to eat. After a few mouthfuls, he noticed that the consistency in his mouth was off. The gristle-like texture forced him to spit out the chunk into the palm of his hand. He looked down and paused in horror, seeing that part of its discoloured innards was a decomposing severed finger. He looked at his grandmother as her lips morphed into a sadistic grin. 'Like I said, Carl, a part of her is still with us.' His stomach churned as he ran through the hallway and out of the house, bolting like the ornamental horse that sat on her fireplace, poised in sprint.

A Grandmother's Inheritance

Marion Bourne sat in her living room watching the tail end of the six o'clock news, blanketed and armed from the plummeting December temperature by her faithful electric fire. The doorbell rang.

Clasping the arm of the chair to pull herself up, she hurried to see who it was, for visitors came sparingly during the winter and nobody liked to be kept waiting. On this occasion, she was sure it was Judith Betler with the charity box from the pensioner's hall, who had said she would be calling this week.

She opened the front door to reveal that there was nobody there. Poking her head outside, her permed white curls fluttering in the passing breeze, she looked from left to right to confirm the absence and locked the door, returning to her TV. Marion thought nothing of it.

'High winds from the north-east tomorrow, with temperatures reach –'

The bell rang again, interrupting the weather forecast. She got up and went to the door in the same manner as before, this time, however, expecting to see a group of youths mischievously running away from the house.

I was a kid once, she thought and smiled quietly to herself as she approached the hallway. Without a peephole or a safety chain, she committed herself again and opened the door. A few cars skimmed past on the main road but there was nobody to be seen on her doorstep. She closed the door, this time assuming that their fun had surely expired and returned to the living room, ready in time for the soap operas.

Before Marion had the chance to begrudge missing most of the televised weather forecast, the doorbell rang for a third time, on this occasion followed by vigorous banging on the door. She paused briefly and rubbed her thumb across the remote control, growing quietly speculative.

Marion got up and opened the door once more. This time, and to her solid expectation after the first couple of nonappearances, she again saw nobody. She walked outside and looked around to certify herself, her arms folded in guard of the cold and her eyes squinting as the leaves brushed up against her.

'Hello?' she called. 'Who's there?'

Sensing the subtle trepidation in her voice, she revised her tone.

'Judith? Is that you?', she exclaimed, this time projecting as if totally absent of fear, though she recognised her anxiety had begun to creep. She felt that calling out a familiar name implied to the persistent knockers, whom she supposed were hiding around the side of the house giggling, that she was expecting someone.

She returned indoors and decisively locked the door, this time settling with the conviction that it wouldn't be re-opened until the bins needed to be placed out the front before bed, regardless of how many times the bell rang, or the door was knocked. Meddling youngsters were sure to have returned home for their supper by then, she thought indignantly. She turned up the volume of her TV – a precautionary measure on the basis that the nuisance knocking would continue, and in so found herself undisturbed for the remainder of the evening in her chair.

Routinely in bed by just after 9pm, Marion simultaneously filled her hot water bottle and gathered the garden shed keys to retrieve the rubbish and place her bags out the front. She walked towards her rear conservatory, opened the door and proceeded outside to unlock the shed. Upon entering, she picked up one of the garbage bags, placing it back onto the floor momentarily after realising its weight. She stood with her knuckles on her hips as she contemplated the mammoth task ahead. As she cerebrated, the shed door swung back open behind her, and with it came a gust of wind, penetrating her skin and forcing the hairs on her arms to stand. *Good job I missed that weather forecast*, she said sarcastically to herself. As she tied the last of the bags, she heard the shed door creak and what seemed to be the resonation of footsteps shuffling behind her. Before she had the chance to turn around, she was on the floor, unconscious.

Marion awoke facing upwards on the garden shed floor, its confined space almost as breath depleting as the weight on top of her.

'Clunk.' A large piece of wood landed on top of the mountain of items already covering her body.

I must have slipped and knocked myself out, she thought at first. Or she had fainted after trying to lift one of the heavier garbage bags. But that didn't explain the haphazard stack of trash, old, shed tools and concrete slabs that were crushing her legs and torso. It seemed as though the shed's entire contents of junk were engulfing her. As she lay almost immobile, but conscious still, her head pulsated violently, and the pain going down her lower back was excruciating.

That ruddy closet, she thought to herself. Continuing to look for a plausible cause, she figured that her deceased husband's wardrobe, which the auctioneer never came to collect after his death the previous year, had fallen on top of her, and with it came an avalanche of the items inside. Yes, that had to be it. Her body frail and her logic scrambled, she tried to exclaim for help, but the jumble on top of her ensured only a whispered cry came out. She could see a half-moon pasted onto the pitch-black sky through the small, shed window and concluded that she must have been unconscious for some time, given her last vivid recollection was switching off the TV after 9pm. Everything subsequently was somewhat of a blur. She wriggled her toes and realised that she was still in her slippers. Her feet were warm, which was a small consolation given the dropping evening temperature and the frigid concrete floor that the back of her body pressed against.

'Crack.' A corded metal appliance hurled upon her, this time a hefty, old fashioned VCR player.

'Help me!' she cried after an in-breath, forced by the increasing weight on her chest. 'Please help me!'

Finally, she had found her voice, a *voice* strong yet laced with a loving and tender intonation even whilst in desperation; a *voice* that had guided her daughters through miraculous childbirth; a *voice* that had once echoed beautifully as a teenager on the old farm grounds whilst calling the sheepdogs, a voice which was, on this occasion, met with no aid. Surely, a neighbour would come. She gave another effort.

And again. And again, to no avail. The shed's items continued to descend and topple upon her, an item here, and an item there, slowly but steadily pressing against her rib cage and stifling her of oxygen.

As the minutes rolled by, Marion tilted her head, as if moving slightly beneath the suffocating rubble would afford her more air. She pushed and pushed with all her might; her ageing, grey frame, trying to recapture the strength of its formative years to cast away the weight that was upon her.

Jackie, Alice and Steven placed one last monstrous concrete slab onto the area covering her chest, securing her agony.

'Goodbye, Granny,' Jackie exclaimed, as the three left the garden shed, their insides smiling as they pondered their inheritance.

The Low-Key Follower

Max put on his coat and swung his backpack around, placing one arm through each strap.

'Promise you'll text me once you're home?' Louise asked, with a perturbed look in her eyes.

'I promise,' Max reassured.

'And you'll kick ass if someone tries to jump you?'

'Wouldn't I always?'

He knew that giving the "tough guy" semblance to Louise was crucial for her peace of mind, as well as the projection of his own masculinity.

'I love you,' she said.

'Oh cheers,' he responded.

Louise slapped at his arm playfully and gave a feigned expression of insult. They laughed and he kissed her gently on the lips before departing.

Max exhaled into his hands as he stood on the outside porch for a moment; pondering the condensation that emanated through his fingers and the two mile walk back to his parents' home. It was a walk he had done dozens of times, but never at this hour. At this very thought, he felt a slight apprehension, probably derived from being told in his childhood "not to go into the dark", just like you "shouldn't talk to strangers". Even at twenty-two, the many proverbs uttered by his good-intentioned parents over the years stayed glued in his subconscious. Nonetheless, he would persevere, as that's what men his age did. The chilly air reddened his cheeks slightly as he lifted his hood and stepped into the November cold.

The streetlights near the large churchyard in which he approached after some ten minutes of walking were mediocre at best, though offered enough glow to navigate passed it. As Max continued on, his peripheral vision caught a crooked-looking figure emerging from the church grounds. He knew the site well as it was the burial spot of his late grandfather, Jim. He was a modest and faithful man, though a little short tempered and a notoriously bad joker. His brother Norman, an army veteran, found him dead in his bed from an overdose of morphine when Max was only six. Sixteen years to the present, the young man's memory of his grandfather had understandably become vague, and he had only his own father to show photographs and relay stories about him.

Max shifted his focus back to his surroundings, though made no attempt to gaze over and profile the shape that had appeared from the churchyard, for staring was blatantly obvious and only showed that he was a little bothered by its presence. But it certainly crossed his mind that to see anybody walking through a cluster of gravestones at 2am must have been unusual. Up until a few moments ago, Max had been contemplating his solitude and thought it brilliant how one could feel so empowered and liberated when walking in the dark. Ah yes – the crisp night air he breathed had been his and his alone; the space he occupied was infinite and the silence to his ears was majestic. And so it was with bitter increased self-awareness that he pulled his hands out of his hoodie muff pocket. His mother's words echoed in his mind: *Walk with your hands in your pockets at night and you're a target's dream*, and she was right. Mothers were always right. But he didn't think to realise that this was the first time he'd actively put her safety advice into practice.

His vigilance had become heightened at the very sight of this strange man, for its large stature and uncannily invasive presence was certainly indicative of a male. As he tried to logically reason its presence – *Why was he also out at 2am? Where was he going? Had he noticed me [Max] on the other side of the pavement?* The man crossed the road, putting himself directly behind Max, at some twenty metres. He felt the innards of his chest dip somewhat as he realised that the figure was now removed from his field of vision, that was unless he turned his head and made it utterly obvious that he was questioning the man's presence. Max felt as though he now only had his ears as a sensor to any form of suspicious behaviour that came from behind him, and if the very worst came to it, he convinced himself, he would either give way to his panic and run; his long, athletic strides would surely take him to safety within mere seconds; or he would be prepared to fight and impale this potential threat with his large house key, which he now held firmly in-between his cold right thumb and index finger.

His mind started to scramble in debating the outward normality of the situation, and the possibility that the man behind him was up to something. He knew that at the surface of it, two men were merely walking in the same direction, on the same pavement, at the same time – a simple concurrence. How idiotic and feeble would he feel and look by breaking the scene's equilibrium and running? But seeds of doubt had their way of manifesting through behaviour, and the last thing he wanted was to appear uneasy. Max kept walking, careful not to yet visibly quicken his pace. Turning his head slightly – just enough as so his peripheral vision caught the figure again, he felt the man was much taller than he, sported a long, black overall and walked with a horrific limp. His left shoulder violently dropped with each step he took forwards, a jarring and mechanical movement that was enough to frighten a small child due to its resemblance to some hideous circus act. Its very motion forced Max to recall the dummies that appeared in the gypsy fairground ghost train during his childhood that never once touched him, but remained etched in his mind long after his mother kissed him good night and closed the bedroom door.

As the minutes rolled by, Max had sensed that the man had drawn a little closer. He knew that he was on St Bernard Street and began to envisage his house, which was tantalisingly no more than four or five minutes away. Soon he would be warm, and out of the presence of this stranger who was rapidly making him perplexed, as well as uneasy. He thought himself: *If someone has a limp, surely it would inhibit walking speed, not increase it?* It left Max in a quandary and thinking of any and all possibilities: was this man who moved so strangely an injured mute that was trying to reach Max for help? Or was he deliberately gaining ground to launch a vicious attack? As he tried to pace his thoughts, he heard what seemed to be sniggering coming from behind him. *A mute? Definitely not.* His instinct began to fear that he was being ridiculed, if not physically targeted. He continued to sense the man's presence edging calculatedly closer behind him.

Within a minute, twenty metres had become ten, ten had become nine and now, he was no further away than five. By this point his biological response to the situation had already been initiated – he needed to act. If he didn't, he would be as useful to himself as a small prey caged with a tarantula, pending consumption.

'Heeheehe,' the mocking giggling behind him transformed uglily into tangible laughter, coupled with a predatory rasp that seemed to reach the back of Max's head.

Max instantly felt his pulse increase, though did his utmost not to show any symptoms of panic. As unpleasantly submerging as it felt, only *he* could bear witness to his own quickening heart – his strides, now fractionally faster, still gave nothing away. As he looked over his shoulder, his pupils dilated at how much the gap between himself and the man had closed. With his head remained turned, looking up, Max could bear witness to only one of the taller man's piercing blue eyes that was saucer wide and made all the more prominent by his blackened surroundings. Alongside his instinctively rising fear, his blood began to simmer at the thought of being preyed upon. And so armed with his key, now slipping in his grip with a little perspiration, he turned around once more, stopped and bravely held his gaze as the man who perused him, white bearded, dishevelled and missing a left eye, drew closer and towered over him.

'Can I help you, mate?' Max uttered.

'Mate, you say? It's uncle Norman to you.'

At 9:05am later that morning, Detective Constable Snow approached her nearest colleague on the corridor.

'PC Evans, you got a minute?'

'Yes, ma'am,' he said.

'You need to see these.' The crime scene photographs showed the corpse of a twenty-two-year-old male on St Bernard's Street with a suspected fatal dose of morphine injected into his system.

Frozen

Billie Turner circled around the ward, feeling it quietly optimistic as she breathed in the clinical air. Her appointment was at 11am, whenever 11am would come, for there were no clocks visible to patients on the ward. Despite their use of fob watches, Billie seldom found herself able to approach the nurses even to ask for the time, or approach anyone in a position of authority for that matter. She felt this to be a shortcoming, but at the same time recognised her great insight by being able to trace such behaviour back as early as her relationships with teachers at primary school, some thirty years ago. But over the last six months, the very absence of clocks on the ward meant that Billie had become more independent in both time telling and time keeping; and had learnt to read the shifting skylight in a bid to estimate the hour for herself. The days were generally boring and somewhat isolating, most of which were spent reading in her room and thinking about her discharge and future outside of the facility.

She continued walking around the ward, and entered one of the lounges, her back cracking slightly as she crouched down to scan the books that were on the lower shelves. It was a long way down, especially for her six-foot, one-inch frame.

She had always known it gave her a decisive physical edge over most of the other patients, even some of the men, but with her size came the inevitable aura of intimidation. But she felt that whilst the vast majority of the nurses and hospital support staff on her ward were fair and empathetic, others had always conspired against her; stereotyping her long and robust stature as being a sure indicator that she had perpetrated her husband's death almost a year ago, in spite of being acquitted. The most notable of persistent underhand mistreatments, Billie felt, came from one of the cooks on the ward, Gerald McClough – a middle-aged, short statured man who she was convinced had sabotaged her birthday celebrations earlier that year. It was only after a slice of the cake was offered to everyone, patients and staff alike looked at one another in unison as they pulled hard, cremated bits of sponge away from their tongues, most of which abandoned their helping after a single bite. McClough's veneer of kindness and long-standing position as a faithful ward cook ensured everyone forgave the apparent mishap, putting it down to accidentally over-baking the cake, but Billie felt the wreck was nothing shy of deliberate.

On the very recollection of food, Billie realised that breakfast had long finished, and she sensed her review with the doctor was approaching. She waited for her name to be called, still scanning the bookshelf in the lounge for something modestly sized to pass the time. *Katherine Knight* or *Yoga for Intermediates*. Both were superficially of interest, but hefty in size and she knew that if she started reading, she would hardly be able to stop – hence the stacks of books in her own room. Nevertheless, she pondered a little, thinking it strange that a psychiatric hospital kept books about infamous killers in view of its patients, many of which themselves had offending histories. Stranger more, she'd never noticed them on the bookshelf, in spite of several close examinations. She picked up *Katherine Knight*, gave a cursory flick through a few random pages, unsure whether or not she wanted to see some gruesome illustration of a man's body. The only man she had ever loved, her husband, was now gone and the subject alone was still as raw as it was a year ago.

'Turner, you're next,' shouted one of the male nurses. Billie closed the book and was escorted out of the ward and to Dr Connolly's office for her monthly review. She always enjoyed the walk, not least of all because she was able to savour what little freedom that the long, relatively spacious corridor offered in comparison to the ward, which at times felt compressed, but also because it indicated that she was one step closer to getting released. She knocked on the door.

'Yes, Billie. Come in,' Connolly shouted.

Billie took a deep breath before entering, for despite his expertise, she was desperate not to be at risk of being misunderstood. She wanted to show that she was in remission, moving on with her life and heading for a much better place. She closed the door behind her.

'Have a seat, Billie.'

She shuffled and sat down opposite him.

'So, how have things been since we last spoke?' he asked. Billie looked upwards, for starting conversations with any man since her husband's death had proven difficult.

'Very well, but I don't want to jinx anything.'

'Have you been taking your medication?'

'Always.'

'That's good. I've heard you've been improving every day since our last appointment.'

'Yes, I've been getting back into the swing of things; playing pool and gardening with Tracy. But I still can't finish that sudoku puzzle you gave me.'

Connolly gave a genuine chuckle, at the same time elongating it to try and encourage further rapport between the pair.

'Is that what you've got there?' he asked.

She looked down and covered the title of the book she had picked up earlier, which was still in her hands. 'Oh, this is nothing' she hedged. 'But I'll keep trying with that sudoku puzzle.'

The doctor laughed. 'Well, I couldn't finish it so I wouldn't fret if you can't either!' he said lightly. He paused for a moment, looking down at the untidy spread of documents that was in front of him on his desk. 'So, let's be serious for a moment. With all things considered, would it be fair to say that you're on the road to recovery?'

'Overall, yes. I mean, I hope so. As I said last time, there's some people here that look at and treat me like dirt. It's really tough to ignore.'

'There'll always be people with a wide range of opinions, Billie. I'm afraid that much you'll never be able to control. Learning to filter out the ones that would impact you negatively is a process in itself.' he said, informatively.

'I know,' she said. 'I can just feel that some people still believe I'm responsible fo –'

'We've exhausted this discussion, Billie,' he interrupted. 'The reason you've been here isn't just because you struggled whilst grieving for your husband, but because the criminal justice system put you through months of turmoil before acquitting you. That much stress could send a person to insanity.'

'I wouldn't say I'm quite that,' she said, giving half a smile.

'And I would agree,' he replied. 'In fact, given your progress over the last few months and what you've told me today, I don't see any further need for you to continue in-patient treatment.'

'You mean … I can go home?' she said.

'Precisely, unless you have any objections, of course. We'll arrange a prescription for you and a nurse to visit you every week, perhaps even fortnightly for the first six months.'

She looked bemuscd in silence for several seconds before generating a response.

'That's … great, I just didn't expect it,' she said.

'I think you probably did,' he suggested, with an admirable look on his face. 'Deep down at least. You're a strong woman, Billie, and maybe now is the time for you to take control of your life once again.'

'So, how soon are we talking? A couple of weeks?'

'Well, there's no time like the present, is there?'

'Today?'

'Today indeed, Billie. If you have to justify it anymore, think of it as an early Christmas present.'

'Crikey. I best get packing then.'

She rose to her feet and gave him a quiet smile of appreciation before turning her head and leaving the office.

After around thirty minutes, she left her room carrying two large bags in her left hand and pulled her suitcase with her right whilst it wheeled behind her. Her taxi was waiting outside to take her home.

'Bye Bill!' several of the patients shouted from the lounge in congruence as she walked passed it. She put her hand up and blew a kiss, repeating the gesture as she continued on past the staff office window. The last room on the right of the corridor before the exit was the kitchen, with which the door was wide open. She knew Gerald McClough was on shift that day as he had served up breakfast for the patients earlier in the morning. As she approached the exit, she found herself stopping before it and looking to her right, at which McClough was inside the kitchen in his apron and looked directly at her.

'I would say congratulations, but your lot go to hell,' he scoffed.

Billie looked behind her, to which nobody was present. She stepped forward into the kitchen, towering enormously over the cook, and whispered, 'At least in hell there's plenty of heat', as she pushed him into the walk-in freezer and slammed the door shut before his desperate screams were muted.

Closing the kitchen door, she left the ward and got into the back of her taxi. It was to be a long journey home, and so she pulled a book from her bag, deliberately skipping the first few pages. '*Katherine Knight…Chapter Two*'

Choking Monopoly

The game had gone on for two hours and thirty-seven minutes. Eliza (daughter) and Coric (father) had been eliminated. It was now a battle between Maggie and Brendon, mother and son.

The mother now held the majority of the properties and had forced Brendon to relinquish most of what he had left.

'Your turn!' she said after moving her piece six places.

Brendon rolled three and landed on Regent Street, a site which had one of his mother's six hotels.

'That's it son, all over,' she said conclusively.

'Wait – I'll mortgage Marylebone Station for £100 and Water Works for…' He looked down at his property card.

'£75.'

'What about that yellow too?'

'Oh yes, mortgage Leicester Square too. £130.'

'That'll give you…' she paused for a moment, as she did the maths on her young son's behalf. '£305 but you owe your mother £1275. You don't have anything else to hand to me so the game is over. I've won.'

'But – what if I just give you the properties without mortgaging them?'

She laughed and looked at her son admiringly, her eyes full of pride at his refusal to succumb. 'Are you trying to tell your ol' mum that one railway station, a utility and a yellow site are worth over £1000? That's scandalous, and you'll have no properties left to play with my boy!' she said.

'I could wait for you to pick the Community Chest card and pay the bucks for all the hotels and houses you've built. That'll even things up.'

'Hmm you were always a little sharper than your sister,' she said with a grin on her face. 'But you're really clutching at straws now … I'll tell you what, if you give me those three sites and your "get out of jail free card" and we'll say no more about it.'

'Deal,' he said. They both looked at each other and smirked at the lenient compromise whilst Brendon handed over his property and "get out of jail free" cards.

Maggie rolled eight and landed on Strand.

She handed the dices to Brendon, at which he rolled six and landed on Park Lane, this time with Maggie's four houses built on it. He looked at his mother.

'Well at least it's a classic way to finish,' she said. 'Landing on the highest colour. Now it's over, okay?'

'It's just not fair,' he said indignantly.

'You know the rules, Brendon, if you're out of the game then you finish by swallowing your piece.'

'But these are sturdier than the Scrabble tiles mum … they won't go down. Dad puked and Eli –'

'Nobody gets anywhere in life without trying son. Your sister and father tried and did so without kicking up a fuss.'

'It's just a game, Mum … plea –'

'Enough. We play by the rules or we don't play at all.'

He placed the ship piece into the back of his mouth, its long, pointed funnels cold and foreign against the base of his tongue, and tried to swallow. He looked across at his deceased sister's little face, which was still blue from her elimination over thirty minutes ago. He started gagging helplessly as the metal piece lodged in his throat. After around a minute of scrambling, the boy fell forward onto the board and passed out.

The mother had won.

The West Bank Mutant

From our bedroom window, I witness the mist of thick clouds shifting across the blackened sky at a moderate pace, covering the full-moon and obliterating any semblance of natural light. The scene, so familiar to me by now, serves as a reminder that dawn will break in as little as two hours. But the daytime no longer offers me the same feeling of safety and security as it had a few days ago.

Now, the extent of my sleep deprivation means that I am etching ever closer to death, but this is a blessing in comparison to falling victim to the gaping jaws of the monstrous beast. The vision of its mouth seems to grow wider and more engulfing by the day, whilst it is my appetite and face that steadily diminishes. I am the meat pending consumption.

Whenever my eyes roll to the back of my head in severe tiredness, there it appears: its robust snout and yellow eyes directly facing me as if poised for an unfair duel, so horrifying that this will mark my fourth consecutive wakeful night. Petrified, I desperately try to remain awake and when my eyes can no longer bear being wide, I have decided that I will end the suffering using my grandfather's old shotgun. It is a death, at least, that doesn't involve falling asleep and feeling its presence, edging ever closer, as I drift deeper into the murky waters of unconsciousness.

It didn't take long for me to deduce that the vision of the creature had come from a trip with my mother to Egypt as a young, twelve-year-old boy. It was here, I bared witness to a large Nile crocodile that was situated in a makeshift zoo. The only thing that separated me from the deadliest predator in the animal kingdom was a thin, flimsy wire fence; incapable of withholding a flock of chickens, let alone a monster from the West Bank. Fortunately, the crocodile seemed old and tired, and probably accepted that it was confined by the very sight of the fence, never to know that a single bite would have dismantled it.

The pond it inhabited appeared uncannily tranquil and steady, as if a man could go edge-side and cup a handful of water to wash his face. It was with this very thought that I saw the snout breaking slowly through the surface of the water, followed by its piercing and prehistoric eyes. Unnervingly slowly, it opened its mouth and bared its set of pointed and disfigured teeth.

But the demon that appears whenever I drift off into a sleep is far more chilling than the beast from the West Bank. Sure enough, a crocodile's jaws are engrossingly unpleasant to look at, not least of all as an intrusive pop-up when you are drifting to sleep. However, this is substantially different. It is a semblance of the massive crocodile I once witnessed, laced with features so disturbing that one could only describe it as some primordial mutation from another dimension. Its teeth, for one, are larger and dirtier, with the spaces that separate them filled with remnants of pink flesh from its last meal. The creature carries with it the very presence of a deeply foreign entity.

Lucy turns around in bed, awoken and aggravated slightly by the tapping of my laptop keyboard.

The doctor has said that I am suffering from "hypnogogic hallucinations": lurking perceptions and sounds that appear as I drift from wakefulness and into sleep. He has prescribed me some sleeping pill that is said to reduce the amount of time it takes to drift off to sleep which I knew wouldn't work, and it hasn't. As dawn starts to break, the clumped, wrinkled duvet and the patterns on the bedroom wallpaper are now sadistically morphing into the shape of snouts and ugly, asymmetrically toothed jaws. The safety I once felt about the daylight is dissipating and it is becoming clear that being awake is no much safer than drifting off to sleep.

I had tried the sleeping pill the previous night and as soon as it began to relax my muscles and guided my eyelids to their desperate closure, the terrorising image would be inserted into my visual field, remaining there until I was fully conscious and alert again. The very thing that tortures me more than any of its physical features is the *stillness* of it. The fact that it can pounce like lightning at any moment, but chooses to remain tantalisingly patient, as if knowing that its very *stillness* evokes just as much fear from me as the prospect of being devoured. The presence is oddly evil, carrying the very aura of a demonic force as if its capabilities extend far beyond a consuming bite.

Lucy gets out of bed and walks towards me whilst I sit by the bedroom window, tapping away.

'You need to sleep, Joe,' she said, perturbed.

'You know that's not possible,' I responded.

She smiled, her mandible strangely pronounced and her cream teeth glistening.

I was still awake, but it had become everything, and everything had become it.

The Forty-Stone Finding

1

It was nearing 4pm and the transitioning sky had begun to initiate its darker tone as Mark Bailey walked through the local funfair with his son, Luca. The peak attendance time had passed, which was corroborated by the fact that a handful of stall holders had already started packing their equipment away, acknowledging that the fairgoers were now coming few and far between.

As they walked through the grounds, glimpsing at stalls and rides from left to right, Mark became enticed by a seemingly large, rustic canopy with "Free Snack Samples" displayed at the head of its entrance. He had yet to eat since breakfast and his son's candyfloss, which Mark had bought for his son two stalls ago seemed rather unappetising, if not somewhat unfair to share.

Luca looked up at his father. 'Can I have money to go on the Dodgems, Dad?'

'What do you say first?'

'Please.'

'Good lad.' He let go of his son's hand and gave the eight-year-old his third five-pound note of the day, after he had earlier dispensed for the candyfloss and a single ride on the Waltzers. 'That's your last one now,' he said, definitively.

'Okay,' Luca said.

'Daddy's going in here for a minute,' Mark said, pointing at the free snack canopy. 'If I'm not by the Dodgems by the time it finishes, come straight back here. I'll keep your candyfloss for you.' He took it with his left hand and his son sprinted to the Dodgems, zigzagging as he avoided the dispersion of people along the way. His father smiled and turned to the canopy.

Mark poked his head through the polyester doorway and entered. He saw a string of tables adjacent to each other with various finger foods placed on their tops. On some of the platters, there were merely crumby remains which he assumed were what had been left by other people. To the left of the food items were a stack of paper plates whilst plastic, white disposable cups filled with cola and cherryade were on the far right. He knew it was neither an exemplary of fine dining nor healthy eating (the opposition being a New Year's resolution he had set himself) but the selection was free, and he had gotten hungrier, which he recognised was made by the sight of the spread that was in front of him.

As he reached for a paper plate to start filling, he heard a light shuffle behind him and turned around to which two large men had appeared, one of which placed a blue cloth over his mouth and nose. Mark gripped the man by the wrist, but it was already too late. The pungent smell of a disinfectant-like substance as he took a scrambling in-breath was so overbearing it started to knock him out. He thought to himself: *chloroform*, as his eyes rolled to the back of his head and his son's candyfloss fell to the floor.

2

Mark awoke flat on his back, raised from the ground and squinting into a bright light which shined directly onto his face. He went to lift his hand to cover his eyes from the light but noticed both wrists were tied to his sides by thick, brown leather straps. After struggling, he gathered himself and looked around hazily, realising he was in what appeared to be an adjustable hospital bed.

'Hi handsome,' a voice said from his left.

He looked and saw a young, blonde woman standing, clothed from head to toe in white, who he assumed, given his clinical-like surroundings, had to be a nurse.

'Where am I?'

'You're in our research facility holding room for the moment,' she said. 'But we'll be transferring you to one of the other rooms tomorrow so we can get started. My name's Nina.'

'Get started? What – How long have I been here?' he asked, discombobulated. 'Those men … knocked me out.'

'You've been here since about five o' clock.'

Mark instinctively looked up for the time and saw 7:35 displayed infront of him on a large corporate looking analog clock face. 'And sorry about Alan and Jerry, they're really

50

quite harmless – it's just how we start recruiting our participants,' she said. She placed a corded remote into his hand. 'Use these buttons to adjust the position of your bed. Helen will be in shortly to explain the proceedings from here. I'll leave you get comfortable.' She walked out.

Mark looked at the remote that had been placed in his right hand and pondered a little. 'Wait…' he exclaimed, but the woman had gone. Starting from left to right, he gave himself a panoramic view of his surroundings, which were just as cold and laboratory-like as his first impression of the place. It took Mark a few moments to come to grips with the fact that the woman he had just spoken to could not have been a nurse, and this place was no hospital.

3

'Hello. HELLO. Anybody!' He gave multiple efforts over the course of around half an hour, but nobody came. He used the buttons on the remote to adjust the bed as so he was sitting upright.

At just after 8pm, Nina returned accompanied by another woman.

'Hi, my name's Helen,' she said, 'I'm the research leader – and you must be … Mark?'

'How do you know my name?'

'Your driving licence gave us the basics,' she said. 'We've also taken your height and weight whilst you were crashed out and are writing up your twelve-month plan as we speak.'

Mark looked utterly bemused. 'I want to know where I am and who you people are!' he asserted. 'Is this a hospi –'

'Definitely not a hospital,' Helen interjected. 'And you're not the first to ask that question. We're in our undercover research facility where you'll be for the next twelve months. Part of our methodology involves gathering subjects which undergo a feeding plan until they reach a target weight.'

'I – my son, where's my boy?'

'He's at home, safe. He started walking back when he realised you were no longer in our tent at the fairground. Don't worry, no harm has come to him, but the police will be out looking for you when your family report you as missing.'

'Is this some kind of a joke?' Mark said. Evidently the shock and disbelief had acted as a catalyst in him coming around from his dazed state. 'Because if it is … show's over. You can undo these straps now and let me the fuck out.'

'Just so we're clear, Mark, we have no interest in inflicting harm on you or your family. The purpose of this study is to monitor and assess the human body's capacity for food. We'll be doing this by focusing on you and the weight you will be gaining over the course of twelve months. It's really that simple.'

Mark laughed. 'Are you honestly taking the piss lady? I know fairs have clowns but whatever this is hasn't got me fooled. Once your joke is over you can undo these straps and I can get back to my family. Bloody idiots.' He turned his head and trailed off.

'In good time. I can see that you're quite agitated at the moment but that'll fade as the days go on. I'll be back tomorrow morning to explain how things are going to work. You should get some rest, you'll be getting a lot of it over the next twelve months.'

'And food,' Nina added. With that, the pair turned on their toes and left the room, which was windowless, and Mark feared soundproof. The bright lights were turned off and he was left to contemplate alone in the dark.

4

Mark shouted intermittently throughout the night, at times exclaiming to use the toilet in the hopes that this was reason enough for the researchers to tend to him. By morning, he had wet himself, and he anticipated seeing the two women again as so he could showcase the mess and point the finger of blame at them. It wasn't until 7am, for then the lights were turned back on and the large clock visible to him, that Helen entered the room with a male assistant.

'Good morning, Mark,' she said. 'This is Ryan.' The male assistant looked at Mark and gave a brief nod.

'How was your first night?' she asked.

'My first night? I've been dying for a piss since you left and nobody came. I want these straps undone so I can go home!' he demanded. 'I've had to piss myself because nobody has been here since last night to let me use the toilet.' He spoke as if to give the impression that he still thought he was in a care facility or a hospital, and that they had a lawful duty of care over him. In his subconscious, however, he feared otherwise. This was some cruel play, and they weren't giving in.

'Ah,' she said. 'We'll get that sorted and change your clothing for you in a little while. Have you got any food allergies or intolerances, Mark?'

'Why does it matter?'

'It's important we know so that we can finish your twelve-month eating plan.'

'Screw your plan. I'll tell you something – undo these straps and I'll tell you anything you want to know.' The sound of desperation had started to creep into his voice as he choked.

'We can't do that just at the moment. But you will need to give us more details sooner rather than later.'

'Or what?' he snapped, indignantly.

'No food.' Ryan said.

'He's right,' Helen said. 'You'll be hungry soon if you aren't already … and if you don't tell us if you have any allergies or if you have any underlying health conditions, then we risk feeding you the wrong items of food.'

'I don't have any goddamn allergies,' he sneered, angry at himself for allowing her to elaborate on and finish her point. 'Thank you. That answers that. What about your general health? Any conditions that we should be aware of?'

'I had asthma as a kid but it's gone now,' he said, reluctantly submitting to her medical-like facade.

'That's fine,' she said looking at Ryan, almost satisfied. 'I guess we can get started by around 9am.'

'Started with what?' Mark asked.

'The feeding,' she said. 'We'll finalise your eating plan in the next hour or so. Like I said yesterday, you're going to be gaining a lot of weight over the next twelve months so you can hit our target weight.'

'What the hell do you mean gaining weight?' he said, 'and what's this thing about twelve months you keep blabbering on about? I want you to let me out of here!'

'You're thirty-four, currently weigh twelve stone and six pounds, and your height is…' She paused, looked at her clipboard '…five foot and eleven inches', which makes your target weight exactly forty stone,' she said, dismissing his plea for freedom.

'Are you trying to tell me that I'm in some sort of fucking feeding clinic?'

'You can think of it like that if it helps,' she said.

'I don't need to gain weight for heaven's sake. Just let me outta here.' He became tearful and exasperated as his masked entreating began to slip.

'You've got to learn to trust us, Mark. We're very experienced researchers and take everything into consideration when it comes to our participants. Your age, height and your weight, as I've just mentioned, gives you a certain target weight. This has often been achieved by other participants before.'

'Other participants?' he responded, with one eyebrow raised and a tear rolling down his cheek. 'You're telling me that you take other innocent people and strap them to beds?'

'We simply do what's necessary in order to yield results for our studies. I'm afraid the nature of the research makes your participation involuntary.'

'So, what are you saying? I have to triple my body weight and then I'll be able to leave here? I've never heard such garbage.'

'Exactly. So, you won't be exercising either. You simply will eat to gain the weight and once you've reached your target in what we hope will be twelve months, you can be rest assured that we'll be letting you go so you can re-join your family.'

Mark looked at her in awe, threw his head back and laughed. 'Nice bloody try.' He tried squeezing out of the straps with a look of contempt and determination on his face.

He stopped after a few attempts, slightly breathless. 'I demand you let me out of these now!'

'I'm going to leave you in the capable hands of Ryan for now, Mark, who'll take you to the treatment room to clean you up and insert a urinary and balloon catheter so you can urinate and defecate freely whilst lying down. Like I said, no exercise for the next twelve months, that includes walking. This bed will be your friend. I'll be back at nine o' clock to see how you're getting on.'

Mark looked up in horror. His palms began to sweat, and his heart palpitated violently. This couldn't have been happening.

5

Ryan disposed of his latex gloves following both procedures. 'All done,' he said. 'So, you like football or?'

Mark said nothing but glanced purposelessly in front of him, clearly traumatised by the probing required to insert both catheters.

'Suit yourself,' Ryan said. 'I'm off now but am back on shift tomorrow morning so we'll catch up then.' He walked out of the room.

It was 8:50am and Mark recalled that Helen would soon be back with more "information", alongside his breakfast. He suspected that the sheer emotional drainage of his situation had given him somewhat of an appetite. Helen entered after a few minutes past 9am, accompanied by Nina who was pushing a large food trolley.

'How are things?' Helen asked, as Nina struggled to push the door closed behind her whilst pushing the trolley.

'Back with more jokes lady?' he said, sardonically.

'We've brought you your breakfast,' she said.

Mark's eyes met the three-tiered trolley once again, which was mounted with an array of calorific, processed foods, including: savoury pies, burgers, pizzas, patties and offensive portions of wedges and chips – every item of food he could see was in multiples, alongside a host of stodgy confectionaries which were on the second tier. All that was visible had been placed on the two upper stands whilst the bottom tier was covered with a white cloth, a mystery that only exacerbated the whirlwind of possibilities in his mind. It was a sheer gargantuan display, enough to bloat a man just be looking at it. But closing his eyes provided little escapism as the very concoctions of smells had soon begun to dance around the room. It was a stench that was impossible to ignore and only as he tried tracing its origins with his eyes that he realised it was emanating mostly from the garlic rice which collided rancidly with its neighbours. The stink of garlic met the salami, which met the Swiss cheese, which then met the fried onions – an overwhelming domino effect that filled him with dread.

'I forgot to mention yesterday, you're expected to comply with each and every feed. Weigh-ins are fortnightly and will involve hoisting you from the bed and onto the scales, which is especially necessary as you get heavier. I'll leave you to it,' Helen said, looking affirmingly at both Nina and Mark before she left. Before Mark had the chance to respond, Nina turned to him.

'Right, shall we get started then?' she said.

Without giving Mark the option of a food, she picked up a large section of pizza, in which its dripping grease qualified the fact that it had been relished with cheese and guided it towards Mark's mouth.

'What do you think you're doing?' he said.

'Before you ask,' she said. 'I can't undo the restraints. My job is to feed you and ensure you eat as much as possible. Now open wide please.'

Reluctantly, Mark opened his mouth and took a bite of the pizza, marking the first mouthful of what would become a living and breathing nightmare.

6

After around ten minutes of eating, Mark swallowed his last piece of pizza and turned his head, gesturing that he was full: 'I'm done.'

'I still don't think you're quite grasping the purpose of the study,' she said, informatively.

'I said I'm done.'

'You think you're going to reach a forty stone target after eating less than half a pizza?'

"The target" and "the study", whenever mentioned, were still like white noise to Mark; concepts that had been mentioned so many times by Helen and Nina since he had been brought to them, yet it seemed as though they hadn't been registered by his conscious mind. He felt that, given his surroundings and general formal approach taken by the assistants: their language, attire and the equipment that they had, he was at best, in an eating disorder feeding clinic, or at worst (given the fact that he was strapped down), had been mistaken for someone on a psychiatric unit.

'I don't understand this "forty stone target" you lot keep going on about. You're mistaking me for somebody else and need to let me go!'

'Helen was quite clear yesterday during your conversation with her, but I'll say it again, just once – our role is to ensure we complete our research into targeted weight gain, and your role is to gain that weight. Until you do, you'll be staying put.'

'I'm full,' he insisted with saucer wide eyes. 'And what you people are doing is unethical!'

'And you're going to feel full. That's the name of the game you idiot,' she snapped, impatiently.

His blood simmered as she went on… 'We haven't even started with the desserts yet,' Nina told him. 'The first feeding is usually the worst, but your stomach will start to enlarge as it gets used to our portion sizes. Now open wide…'

'I've had enough! I'm not eating anymore,' he said with conviction. He smacked his lips and looked directly in front of him, as if he'd physically put a barrier between Nina and himself that prevented her from feeding him any further.

'This isn't even close to being good enough.' She came at Mark's mouth, this time switching to a syrup coated pastry, but he had momentarily conjured up a plan to retaliate. He opened his mouth, chewed on the pastry and pretended to swallow. As Nina bent forward with yet another segment, he violently spat upwards, catching her directly on her face.

'You bastard,' she exclaimed, wiping her eyes with her sleeve. She slapped him across the face. He reddened, and his eyes started welling up at the very recognition of his turmoil, as well as the sharp sting of her hand. He thought that the incident would at least diffuse being force-fed any further, but Nina remained committed. She reverted to what she had fed him first – the pizza, tormentingly picking up another slice and looking at him. 'We'll start again then shall we,' she said, with a pretence patience to her voice.

Forced to comply, and after two hours of feeding, Mark felt sick to his stomach. He had already consumed enough to fill a small horse and the very prospect that there was more to come later in the afternoon and in the evening was beyond daunting.

He started heaving profusely, followed by a spout of vomit.

'I can't take anymore. I'm begging you. Please stop.'

7

As the months rolled by, Mark lie in his bed and repeatedly tried raising his head, his strength and willpower tucked underneath pound after pound of fatty flesh.

'Twenty-three stone and four pounds,' Helen said. 'We've got until February the third until your last weigh in. That's another sixteen weeks.'

'And if I'm not forty stone by then, what happens?' he asked.

'Participants don't leave until they've reached the target that they've been set, regardless of how long it takes. It's one of the study's necessities.'

A single teardrop fell from his eye as he wheezed heavily and slowly began to realise, he wasn't getting out alive.

A Glimmer of Hope

Twenty-nine-year-old Sandra sat in her middling block flat, snuggling into her boyfriend's chest as they braced the penetrating night-time January conditions. They were now out of gas and hadn't been able to afford to top the heating up since the previous month, which was characterised by the condensation dripping down the living room window.

'Mum, when's dinner ready?' Milo shouted from his bedroom.

Sandra and Dom's food cupboards were empty and what little money they had left had been spent on a taxi to drive them back from hospital two days ago. Sandra had then given birth to their third child, Sammy.

'You know that we've got nothing for tonight. Go back to bed please.'

'We had nothing last night either!' Milo quipped. 'Me and Violet are hungry.'

'I said back to bed.'

Sandra and Dom sat on the couch whilst they listened to Milo sob due to his second night without any supper. Going to bed on empty, rumbling stomachs wasn't easy for the parents, let alone the growing frames of twelve-year-old Milo and five-year-old Violet. Sammy, the new-born, lie blanketed, asleep in his car seat on the living room floor; his father rocking it back and forth with his foot in order to prevent him from feeling the chilly air that reddened his little cheeks.

Dom turned to his girlfriend. 'Milo ain't gonna settle again tonight. He's starving.'

'What the hell are we going to do?' asked Sandra. 'They can't go another night without food.'

'None of us can,' Dom responded, sighing as his eyes closed in exhaustion.

Sandra observed his thinning face; and was reminded of the fact that he had barely slept since Sammy's birth and, just like the rest of them, had not eaten since being at the hospital. A middle aged, kind-hearted nurse on the ward, Myrtle, had quietly broken policy whilst Sandra and the family were on the maternity ward for over four days. Realising the family's struggles, she would return from the staff kitchen with ham sandwiches, biscuits and squash for Dom and the children as they supported Sandra during her labour. She would never express that she had been infertile her entire life and so chose to surround herself with children by working on a maternity ward. But now Sandra and Dom had returned home, they were alone in their hunger and desolation.

Sandra reached for her purse and peered inside, displaying a host of maxed out credit cards and a trivial amount of copper change. They looked at their tiny, blue and tan dog that sat on the floor and then at each other.

Sandra walked into the kitchen, opened the door and placed the Yorkshire Terrier inside. Her heart started pounding as she turned the dial to 180 degrees and wiped a tear that rolled down her cheek. Walking back into the living room, she sat back down on the sofa and placed both hands over her ears, blocking out the desperate sound of whimpering that came from the oven.

They would eat tonight.

With his head in both palms, despondent, Dom opened his eyelids and peered between his fingers for several seconds, hoping for some divine intervention that could fix their despair. Looking at the thin shawl that covered the sleeping newborn, he noticed what appeared to be the corner of a brown envelope erupting from Sandra's hospital toiletry bag on the floor.

'What's that?' Dom observed, leaning forward for a closer look.

'What's what?' Sandra replied, keeping one hand clasped over her right ear.

He bent forward a little further and pulled the envelope, which had been sealed, from the bag and brought it in closer view of Sandra and himself. Looking at each other, both puzzled, he teared it open and pulled out a folded, white piece of paper which had on it handwritten in black ink:

I hope the contents of this envelope will help you, at least for a while, find some comfort and relief as you bring this beautiful new life into the world. God Bless you. – M

The pair then turned to the envelope once more, before Dom started pulling out neat piles of ten and twenty-pound notes. They paused at each other's eyes for a moment, lost for reason, before Dom drew himself back into his surroundings and pointed his finger violently towards the kitchen, 'Get him out!'

Sandra turned on her toes and re-opened the oven door, quickly pulling the terrier out and drawing him close to her chest.

'How much is in that thing?' she asked, standing up and her eyes moon wide.

It took Dom another half a minute to flick through the remaining notes, his lips moving as he ensured that his counting was accurate. They both looked at each other in awe as the dog, still warm from moments prior, trustily licked her face.

'Two grand,' he replied.

'All from that nurse? But why would she…?'

'God knows,' he said. 'And I don't think she'd want us to waste time questioning it.'

Sandra walked back into the living room, placed her hand on the banister and shouted up the stairs. 'Kids, come here.'

Milo and Violet raced across the landing and stood atop the stairs.

'Who wants a takeaway?' she asked, enthusiastically. They looked at their mother and smiled whilst Myrtle, some fifty miles away and alone in front of her TV, found herself smiling too.